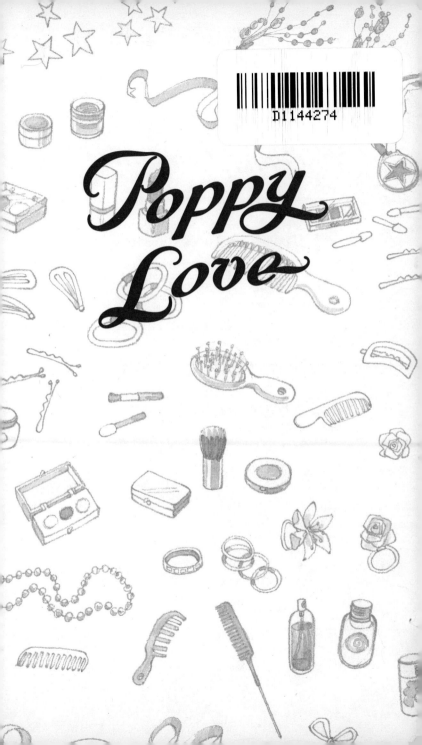

Poppy Love

Poppy Love titles

Poppy Love Steps Out

Poppy Love Faces the Music

Poppy Love Rock 'n' Roll

Poppy Love Star Turn

Poppy Love In the Spotlight

Poppy Love Tango Queen

Poppy Love Goes for Gold

Poppy Love
All That Jazz

NATASHA MAY

illustrated by
SHELAGH McNICHOLAS

WALKER
BOOKS

With thanks to Neil Kelly and the students of
Rubies Dance Centre
N.M.

With thanks to Carolyn, Julia, Kirsty and Ann at
Bell's Dance Centre
S.M.

First published 2010 by Walker Books Ltd
87 Vauxhall Walk, London SE11 5HJ

2 4 6 8 10 9 7 5 3 1

Text © 2010 Veronica Bennett
Illustrations © 2010 Shelagh McNicholas

The author and illustrator have asserted their moral rights
in accordance with the Copyright, Designs and Patents Act 1988

This book has been typeset in ITC Giovanni

Printed and bound in Great Britain by Clays Ltd, St Ives plc

British Library Cataloguing in Publication Data:
a catalogue record for this book is available from the British Library

ISBN 978-1-4063-2024-4

www.walker.co.uk

Contents

Summer School

Along with her partner, Zack Bishop, and their friends, Poppy went to dance lessons every week at the Blue Horizon Dance Studio. She and Zack had done well in competitions, both in the seaside town of Brighton, where they lived, and further away. In fact, they had recently won a big competition involving children from all over Great Britain!

It was Friday afternoon. On Monday it would be Poppy's birthday, and the start of the summer holidays.

"Wow! I can't believe this year's gone already!" said Poppy to her friend Mia Porter as they waited at the gate for Mrs Porter. Poppy's family owned a hotel, and as Poppy's mother worked there every day while her dad worked in London, Mia's mum collected both girls.

"Me too," agreed Mia. "And it was the busiest year ever! Look, there's Mum."

As they walked home, Poppy thought about how busy the year had been. Apart from everything she'd done at school, she and Zack had performed in lots of shows, competitions and dance exhibitions all over the south of England and in Blackpool, the ballroom dancing capital of Great Britain. Also, Poppy's Auntie Jill, who used to be a ballroom dancing champion herself, had met Uncle Simon and got married to him. All in the space of a year!

"It's Poppy's birthday on Monday," Mia said to her mother.

"Of course!" said Mrs Porter. "Are you having a party?"

"Not this year," Mia reminded her. "Poppy's mum and dad are taking us to see a film tomorrow instead."

"Oh yes," said Mia's mum. "Now I remember."

Poppy's parents had been so busy lately, there had been no time to organize a party, especially on the first day of the holidays, when so many of Poppy's friends would be going away. "I don't mind," she told Mrs Porter. "I'm starting a dance summer school on Monday. That's my big present."

"Goodness!" exclaimed Mrs Porter. "Don't you need a rest?"

"Summer school's only for two weeks," Poppy explained. "And it's just as much fun as a holiday, learning all kinds of dance. Zack and some of my other friends from Miss Johnson's are coming – and Auntie Jill's a guest teacher. We get to do a show at the end, too."

"It sounds like you'll have a great time doing what you love best, Poppy," said Mrs Porter.

When they reached the Gemini Hotel, Poppy said goodbye and ran up the steps. "Mum, I'm home!" she said, pushing the glass door.

"See you tomorrow, Poppy!" called Mia, waving as she and her mum walked on. "And happy birthday!"

Burne Hall was a boarding school where children learned dancing, music and acting. In the holidays no one was there, so the studios were free for summer schools. There was also a theatre, a big gymnasium, buildings where the boarding pupils slept, and ordinary classrooms too.

"Oh good," said Zack on the first morning, looking at the list of classes on the wall. "We've got tap dancing with Miss Ford."

He and Poppy already knew Miss Ford because one of her Burne Hall pupils, Nick Price, came to Miss Johnson's Competition Class at the Blue Horizon. "Miss Ford's so nice!" agreed Poppy.

Just then their friends Sophie and Sam arrived. "If we can't do this tap dancing stuff, do you think we can just go home?" Sophie asked Poppy nervously.

But she needn't have worried. Miss Ford, who wore her red hair in a pony-tail and had freckles on her nose, gathered the children around her in a circle. "This isn't school, it's *summer* school," she said. "So let's have some fun!"

She counted twenty children in the circle, fifteen girls and five boys. "We'll go round the circle, each of you saying your name, and I'll see how many I can remember," she said. "Then you can try. Cheating allowed, of course, especially if you already know each other!"

The children had fun playing the name game. Poppy tried to sort everyone out, but it was hard. There were two Matthews, and girls called Lucy, Louise and Laura, all three

with light brown hair. Zeenat was a slim girl
with golden brown skin and a long plait, and
Marsha wore a bright yellow leotard and had
the longest legs Poppy had ever seen. But
who came next? A tall girl with her dark hair
in a bun, whose name Poppy just *couldn't*
remember.

"Now," Miss Ford was saying, "hold
hands with the person next to you and put
your right foot forward." She looked at the
children's feet as they did this. "I can see one
left foot," she said.

It was Sam's. He hopped on to the other
one, grinning, and the class started. They
learnt how to do a shuffle, where the foot
brushes the floor, toe to heel, and then
practised the step in time to music. Miss
Ford showed them how to step to the side,

cross their foot over, bring their leg round and "tap!" smartly on the floor. There was a lot of giggling and teasing, but by the end of the class they were able to copy Miss Ford in a short step sequence.

"Give yourselves some applause," said Miss Ford, clapping her hands. "You've done really well!"

And they'd enjoyed themselves too.

"Ballroom this afternoon!" said Sam happily when they broke for lunch.

"No showing off, Sam, just because it's Poppy's auntie teaching us," warned Sophie, who knew her partner well.

"Would I show off?" asked Sam innocently, spreading his hands.

"Yes!" said Sophie, Poppy and Zack all together.

Auntie Jill didn't treat Poppy any differently from the other children. "We're starting with the cha-cha-cha," she told the class after the warm-up. "Those of you who've done ballroom dancing before can partner the beginners. But let's start by learning the steps individually. Find a space and watch me."

The children copied what she did. The cha-cha-cha was a good dance to start a new class with because it didn't need much space, and you could do it without a partner while

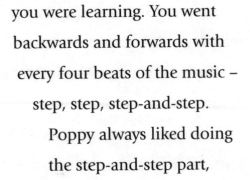

you were learning. You went backwards and forwards with every four beats of the music – step, step, step-and-step. Poppy always liked doing the step-and-step part,

a little hip-swivel that fitted
with the rhythm of Latin
American music.

"This is my favourite dance," said
one of the two boys called Matthew.

"You've never, ever danced
before!" pointed out another boy
whose name Poppy didn't know.
He looked so like Matthew, though, she
thought they might be brothers.

"Don't care," replied Matthew, cha-cha-
cha-ing confidently. "I love it!"

"That's excellent," said Auntie Jill. "Do you
want to try doing it with partners?"

"Yes!" called out several of the
children.

"Can I dance with Matthew?" asked
Zeenat. "He's so good, and I'm terrible!"

Poppy had noticed that Zeenat hadn't picked up the step very well. Sometimes her little hop wasn't on the right bit of the music, or she missed it altogether. Auntie Jill pondered for a moment, then put her hand on Zack's shoulder. "Suppose you dance with Zack, Zeenat?" she said. "Matthew's learning quickly, but Zack knows this dance very well." She turned to Matthew, who was looking disappointed. "Why don't you dance with Sophie?" she suggested. "She's just the right height."

Poppy danced with the girl called Laura because there weren't enough boys to go round. Laura looked at her feet, biting her bottom lip. Most of the time, all Poppy could see of her was the top of her light brown hair.

"Try and look up, Laura!" called Auntie Jill.

"Don't worry, Poppy won't step on your toes!"

After a little while they changed partners. Poppy danced with the dark-eyed girl who wore her hair in a bun. She turned out to be called Susanna, and seemed to be a natural dancer. "You're good at this!" said Poppy.

"Thanks," said Susanna quietly. "I've done a bit of ballroom before. I've done a bit of everything, really."

Then something peculiar happened. Poppy found her hand taken by Auntie Jill, who apologized to Susanna and led Poppy to the front of the room. "Come along," she said, "you and I are going to show the class how to do a New York."

The New York was a step in the cha-cha-cha. Poppy was mystified. Auntie Jill had promised not to single her out in class, and she always kept her promises. So what was she doing?

Poppy turned to face the class, her cheeks very pink. Sam had said he wouldn't show off, and here was Poppy, doing exactly that!

Then something even more peculiar happened. The studio door opened, and everyone in the room starting singing. To Poppy's astonishment, Miss Johnson walked slowly in, carrying a large pink-and-white birthday cake with the candles lit.

"Happy birth-day, dear Poppy," sang the children. *"Happy birth-day to you!"*

Auntie Jill folded back a partition wall. Behind it there was a long table, decorated with streamers and balloons, and laid with a delicious tea. Miss Johnson put the cake in the middle.

"Come on, birthday girl," she said to Poppy. "Time to blow out your candles and make a wish."

Poppy had forgotten all about her birthday! She was so surprised, her feet seemed stuck to the floor. Zack took one arm and Auntie Jill the other, and they led her to the table. In a daze, Poppy made a wish and blew out the candles. Then Auntie Jill put her arm round her shoulders. "It was Sarah's idea," she told her. Sarah was Miss Johnson.

"But Jill did most of it," said Miss Johnson.

"And no one else knew," added Auntie Jill. "Not even your mum and dad!"

Poppy felt shy, but very happy. "Thank you, everyone!" she said. "Um…" Then she couldn't think of anything more to say, and everyone laughed.

"Who wants to eat?" asked Miss Johnson. "Apart from Sam, of course!"

The children gathered round the table, and the cha-cha-cha lesson was forgotten as the food disappeared.

"How's summer school been so far?" Miss Johnson asked Poppy and Zack, handing them slices of cake.

"Brilliant!" declared Zack. "I even managed not to fall over in the tap dancing class!"

"And what about you, Poppy?" asked their teacher.

Poppy thought, licking icing off her fingers. "Summer school's great," she said. "And this has definitely been the best birthday I've ever had!"

Susanna's Secret

Poppy was enjoying summer school, though learning so many new steps was hard work. This morning, they were going to meet a new teacher, Mr Cheshire, who taught jazz dance.

Jazz turned out to be unlike anything else they'd ever done. You didn't have to point your feet and follow exact lines, like in ballet. And it wasn't like tap either, which was full of steps, steps, steps. In jazz, the moves took

up your whole body, and you could do them your own way, or even invent new ones.

Mr Cheshire wasn't very tall, but he was as strong and energetic as an acrobat. "Jazz is fun," he told the children, "but you have to keep your middle strong, or it looks *terrible*." He rolled his eyes, and the children laughed. "And no one stays terrible for long in my class!"

They did their warm-up, then Mr Cheshire put on some music and turned the volume up. Poppy was thrilled by the sound. It wasn't like ballroom-dancing music or tap music. It had someone singing in a raspy voice, as if they had a sore throat, and behind the singing was a strong drumbeat that made Poppy want to get up and move, *now*.

"Follow what I do," called Mr Cheshire

over the music, "and most important, relax!"

Maybe *that* was the secret of jazz, thought Poppy. Mr Cheshire's movements looked as free as flowing water. Eager to learn, she copied him carefully, trying hard to hold her tummy firm yet make her movements relaxed.

They learnt the jazz square, keeping their knees loose as they stepped and crossed, stepped and crossed their legs. They moved their hips and chests forward and back, rolling their heads, using every inch of their body. Mr Cheshire even showed them how to moonwalk – to walk backwards but look as if you're walking forwards. Sam was so excited about this, Poppy thought he was going to burst.

"Now the real fun starts," announced Mr Cheshire. "Use the moves you know, make some up and put them together. We call it improvisation!"

Poppy listened to the music, wondering what to do. She watched Susanna, who had obviously done jazz before, throw herself into her dance sequence. She seemed to forget everything around her as she twirled and leapt, linking her movements with no stops and starts. Some of the things she did looked difficult, but they fitted into the improvisation smoothly.

Poppy started off by copying Susanna, but she soon lost herself in her own improvising. It felt

great to have the freedom to move
her entire body, stretching
and pulling, kicking and
crouching. By the end of the
class Poppy felt tired, but there
was no doubt about it – she
absolutely *loved* jazz!

Outside the studio, Zack and Susanna
were looking at the list of classes on the wall.
"Ballet this afternoon," Poppy read from the
list. "With Mr Cheshire again."

"You'll be brilliant at that, I bet," said
Susanna. "Since you're brilliant at everything
else."

Poppy was astonished. "But so are you,
Susanna!" she pointed out.

"Well, I told you," said Susanna. "I've done
a bit of everything."

Her dark eyes looked serious, and she wasn't smiling. In fact, the only time Poppy could remember seeing her smile was during the surprise birthday party yesterday. She didn't seem to be enjoying summer school much.

"What's ballet like, Susanna?" asked Zack.

Susanna picked up her bag. "Why don't you just wait and see, like everyone else?" she said. "I'm going to have my lunch now."

When she'd gone Zack gave Poppy a puzzled look. "Did I say something wrong?" he asked.

Everyone's family and friends were invited to the summer school show. Poppy was excited about all the routines they were preparing, but she was especially thrilled when Mr Cheshire beckoned to her at the end of a jazz class one morning, and said, "Would you like to do a jazz solo in the show, Poppy? You're good enough."

Poppy's face felt hot. "But I've never done jazz before this week!" she said.

"Then you're even better than I thought," said Mr Cheshire, grinning as he left the studio.

Zack was smiling with his whole face. "Awesome, Pop!" he said.

"Wow!" cried Sophie, hugging Poppy. "You deserve it!"

"Come on, it's lunchtime," said Sam. "If we don't hurry there'll only be salad left."

But as Poppy was following the others out of the studio, she suddenly caught sight of Susanna sitting on the floor, half-hidden by

the piano in the corner. She had her hands over her face, but Poppy could tell she was crying.

"I'll catch you up," she said to her friends, and knelt beside Susanna. "What's wrong?" she asked.

"Go away," came Susanna's voice from between her fingers.

Poppy didn't know what to do. Could Susanna be jealous of her because of the jazz solo? But Mr Cheshire had given Susanna the main part in the ballet routine. In fact, every child had been given something special to do, however small.

When Susanna raised her head, Poppy saw how red and troubled her eyes were. She felt very sorry for her. "Why are you crying?" she asked again.

Susanna bit her lip. "My mum and dad are both dancers," she said.

"That's nice," said Poppy uncertainly.

"No, it's *not* nice!" retorted Susanna. "It's awful. They want me to be good enough to dance professionally!"

"But you *are* good," pointed out Poppy.

Susanna shook her head impatiently. "The thing is, to be a dancer you've got to *want* to be a dancer. But I don't think I *do*! I don't care if I never perform again." Once more she began to cry. "But I can't tell my parents that!"

Poppy thought about how Auntie Jill, who was also a dancer, always encouraged her in her love of dance, but never said anything about wanting Poppy to be a professional dancer. It was Poppy herself who had decided that.

"They'll be so disappointed, Poppy," said Susanna, sniffing.

No wonder Susanna was unhappy, feeling these things but having to keep them secret. Poppy touched her hand. "Listen," she said, "I've got an idea."

Susanna looked at her in surprise. "What is it?" she asked.

"I'm going to talk to my Auntie Jill," replied Poppy.

Poppy loved the costume for the jazz routine, with its short skirt and sparkly top. But she liked the floaty skirt she was wearing in the ballet piece too. And she wasn't nervous before the show. She was having such a great time at summer school, she was sorry it would soon be over.

"Are your parents here?" she asked Susanna, who was waiting beside Poppy in the wings. With her hair in a bun and her dark eyes made up with eyeliner, Susanna looked beautiful in a white tutu, pink tights and satin ballet shoes.

"Yes," she said. "Are yours?"

Poppy nodded. "And my brother Tom, and Zack's mum, and my friend Mia and her mum. They wouldn't miss it!"

The show was about to start. Poppy and the other girls took up their positions. The curtains parted. Susanna ran on, the audience applauded and the music began. The lights on the stage were too bright for Poppy to see her family, but she knew they were there.

After the ballet, they did the ballroom routine Auntie Jill had made up. It was

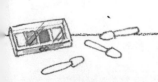

33

a waltz, with the dancers swirling in circles and crossing in lines. Each girl had a different colour dress, and each boy wore black trousers and a shirt. Auntie Jill had given special parts to the less experienced dancers, who had worked so much harder than Poppy and her friends from the Blue Horizon Dance Studio. And everyone, to Poppy's relief, danced beautifully.

During the five boys' tap dance, one of the Matthews – Poppy still wasn't quite sure which was which – fell over, got up and joined in again without missing a beat, which got a round of applause. And the

audience clapped even louder when the fifteen girls, dressed in sparkly leotards and shiny tights, joined the boys and tap-tap-tapped their way through Miss Ford's lively routine.

As Poppy changed into her jazz costume, she wished that the last day of summer school could last for ever. But although she knew it couldn't, the friendships she had made in the last two weeks *definitely* would.

The fast, spectacular jazz routine was the finale of the show.

"Ready, everyone?" said Mr Cheshire as they lined up for their entrance. "This is the best routine I've *never* choreographed, so make sure you dance your socks off!"

The children laughed. The jazz routine had been worked out by Susanna. She had taught them the moves, patiently showing them what to do, correcting and helping them, and all the time weaving the steps into a stunningly entertaining routine.

The jazz music began, filling the theatre with a thudding beat, and lights came on, flooding the stage with colour. The audience whooped as Poppy and the others bounded on, putting all their energy into performing Susanna's piece as well as they possibly could. Poppy knew it looked great, and when the spotlight landed on her she did her solo better than ever before.

At the end the audience applauded for so long that Miss Ford had to wait, the microphone in her hand, to make her announcements.

"Many thanks to the teachers, the parents and of course the children themselves," she said, beaming at the audience. "Now, Mr Cheshire has asked me to make a special announcement. Would Susanna Wellstone please come up?"

Susanna's cheeks were very pink as she made her way across the stage. Poppy noticed a smartly dressed couple in the front row, whispering to each other. They must be Susanna's parents.

"Susanna has proved not only a fine dancer this week," said Miss Ford to the audience, "but an excellent choreographer.

She made up the jazz routine you have just enjoyed, which for a girl of her age is very advanced work indeed. Will you join me in giving her a special round of applause?" The audience roared and clapped, but on their feet, and clapping louder than anyone else, were Susanna's mum and dad.

Susanna ran and caught hold of her parents' hands, pulling them towards where Poppy stood with Mum and Auntie Jill. "Come and meet Poppy," she urged them. "It was all her idea!"

Poppy felt shy. "My auntie did it, really," she told them. "She asked Mr Cheshire if Susanna could make up the jazz routine."

"And I so loved doing it!" added Susanna, her eyes shining.

Susanna's mother, who was very elegant, with her hair swept into a roll on the back of her head, put her arm around her daughter's shoulders. "We never knew how clever you were at making up dances, Susie," she said.

"It was brilliant," added her dad.

Poppy could see how proud they both were. But she was proud of her auntie too, for helping to make it happen.

Then, just when Poppy thought today must be perfect, something else happened. Mum and Auntie Jill exchanged a look. "Shall we tell her?" asked Mum.

"Why not?" replied Auntie Jill.

"Poppy, we're going on holiday!" said Mum, with excitement in her eyes.

"To France. We leave the day after tomorrow."

"Cool!" cried Poppy. Then she thought of something. "But what about the hotel?"

"Uncle Simon's going to help Jill look after the hotel," explained Mum. She smiled happily at Poppy. "He calls it 'going on holiday to the Hotel Gemini'."

"Summer school and a holiday as well," said Poppy, still with her arms around her mum. "What a great summer this is!"

And best of all, as she and Zack said goodbye to their new friends from summer school, Susanna hugged them both. She didn't say anything, but on her face was the biggest smile Poppy had ever seen.

The Red,
White and Black Dance

Poppy had never been abroad before. She
and her brother Tom were so excited that
Mum asked Tom to sit in the front of the car,
while she sat beside Poppy on the back seat.
"You two are like little bottles of pop!" she
said. "Now calm down!"

It was hard to calm down, though. The
ferry with its echoing, petrol-smelling car
deck, its bars, restaurants and rows of seats

was unlike anywhere Poppy had ever been before. She felt the hum of the engines beneath her feet and watched the water churning behind the ship as it made its way towards the French coast.

Dad pointed on the map to the very bottom corner of France. "The villa we've rented is down here in the south, near Spain," he told them.

"Wow!" said Poppy in surprise. "France is *huge*!"

"It'll be a long journey," said Mum.

"I think I'd better sit in the back of the car again, don't you?"

When they drove off the ferry Poppy was amazed. "It's not like Brighton," she said.

"Duh! That's 'cos it's *France*," said Tom, though he was peering out of the car windows just as eagerly as his sister.

The grey buildings had tall windows with shutters on the outside and lace curtains on the inside. There were towns with cobbled squares and cafés with outdoor tables, and miles of straight roads  between fields and lines of trees. When it got dark, the Loves stopped at a hotel with hard, sausage-shaped pillows on the beds, and set off again the next morning.

The long journey was worth it. When at last they got out of the car, hot and stiff-legged, Poppy thought she had never seen a prettier house than their little white villa, covered with flowers.

"It's like a doll's house!" she said.

It had tall windows at the front and, Poppy and Tom soon discovered, glass doors at the back that led to a terrace and a fenced garden with a swimming pool. "Mum!" called Tom. "Can we go in the pool?"

Mum found their swimming things and the bottle of sunblock, and Poppy and Tom jumped in and splashed around while Mum and Dad unpacked the car. Then they came out of the house and sat at the table on the terrace. "This is the life," said Dad, stretching.

Just then, they heard
a voice calling, "Hello!
Hello!"

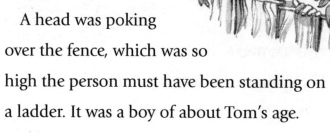

A head was poking
over the fence, which was so
high the person must have been standing on
a ladder. It was a boy of about Tom's age.

"Hello!" called Dad in reply. "Are you
English?"

"No, I am French," said the boy. "My name
is Fabian. This is my house."

The way he spoke didn't sound *quite*
like English usually did, but it was easy to
understand him. "You speak good English,
Fabian," said Mum.

"I learn in school," said the boy.

Tom was learning French at school, but
Poppy knew he would be too shy to speak it.

"My name's Poppy," she told the French boy. "And this is my brother, Tom."

"Poppy and Tom," repeated the boy. *"Bienvenue!"*

"That means 'welcome'," said Mum to Poppy and Tom. To Fabian she said, *"Merci, Fabian!"*

"That means 'thank you'," Tom told Poppy importantly.

A girl's face suddenly appeared beside Fabian. She was younger than him, and had almost-black hair, cut in a straight fringe. "Josette!" she announced. Then she said something in French to Fabian.

"She is my sister," he told them. "She wants to say hello to Poppy."

"Hello, Josette!" called Poppy, and the two girls smiled at each other.

"Do you like swimming?" she asked Josette.

Neither Josette nor her brother seemed to understand, so Poppy mimed swimming movements and pointed to the pool.

"Ah, yes!" exclaimed Fabian. "Thank you! We come?" he asked Mum.

Mum nodded, laughing. "Ask your parents first!" she told them.

The two faces disappeared, and five minutes later the children returned in their swimming costumes, with towels under their arms.

It didn't seem to matter that Fabian and Josette spoke a different language. Swimming was fun without the need for any words. While they were in the pool, their mother, who said her name was Mimi, came over with drinks on a tray, and they all gathered round the table.

Mimi, who had her hair tied up with a scarf and wore sunglasses, spoke English. She told Poppy's parents she was very glad the Loves were renting the villa. "In June and July, only old people stay here," she said. "But now it is August, and children come."

"It's nice for Poppy and Tom to have Fabian and Josette next door too," said Dad.

"What do Poppy and Tom like to do?" asked Mimi. "Fabian likes very much to play tennis."

"I like football," said Tom, "but tennis is all right too."

"And Poppy's happiest when she's dancing," said Mum.

"Dancing!" exclaimed Mimi, taking off her sunglasses and looking at Poppy with bright eyes. "Josette too! She likes to do the … I don't know the English word … *Danse Basquaise*."

"Basque dancing?" said Mum, looking interested.

"*What* dancing?" asked Poppy. It sounded like "bask". But basking was sunbathing, not dancing!

Dad leaned forward. "This part of France is near Spain," he explained. "Just over the border is the area where the Basque people live, and many of them live over here in France too. They speak Spanish or French these days, but there is an ancient Basque language, and the Basque traditions are still kept up."

"But we're still in France, aren't we?" asked Poppy, feeling slightly confused.

"Yes," said Dad. "The Basque people don't have a separate country. They're a bit like Welsh and Scottish people at home, who live in Great Britain but have their own languages and traditions."

Mimi murmured something to Josette in French, and Josette nodded enthusiastically.

"Josette's Danse Basquaise group will be dancing in the market square on Wednesday," said Mimi. "Would Poppy like to join them?"

"Would I!" echoed Poppy. "But I don't know the steps."

"Josette's teacher will show you," said Mimi. "You will learn quickly."

Poppy smiled at Josette. "Yes, please, then!" she said.

"That's our Poppy!" said Dad, laughing. "Always dancing, even on holiday!"

* * *

Everything to do with the Basque country was red, white and black, with touches of green: the flags, the flowers and decorations in the streets, the window displays in the shops, the local sports teams' kits. And so were the Basque dancers' costumes.

The girls wore full red skirts, white blouses and black waistcoats. On their heads were white lacy caps, and they had white socks and black shoes.

Poppy felt very important as she joined the line of dancers, adults and children, walking out into the middle of the square.

All around them were crowds of local people and holidaymakers, holding up cameras and carrying their small children on their shoulders. It was hot and noisy, and the air was full of the delicious smells of barbecuing food.

As well as Poppy's group, there were women dancers in long skirts, and men in white trousers and shirts, with red scarves around their waists. The music was played by two men, one with a drum and one with a pipe that made a high, sad sound, like someone singing without words. They too were dressed in Basque national dress. It was all so colourful and lively, Poppy could see

why the dancing attracted so many spectators.

"Lots of people!" she said to Josette, pointing to the crowd.

"*Oui*," agreed Josette. "*Oui*", which sounded like "oo-ee", was the French word for "yes". "Pee-pull," she added, copying Poppy.

"*Oui!*" said Poppy happily.

The first dance was done by teenage girls. They stood in lines, weaving between one another or moving backwards and forwards, pointing their toes and doing little jumping steps. In one dance they held their arms above their heads, and in another they swung their legs out to the side. Poppy thought they danced very gracefully.

Then it was Poppy's big moment. Lucien, the grey-haired man who taught the dancing, handed the girls garlands made of red, white and green paper flowers. They stood in two lines, facing each other, and began to do the flower dance.

Poppy had found it quite complicated at the first class she had attended with Josette, just two days earlier. She'd had to learn to hold first one, then the other, end of the U-shaped garlands, passing them from hand to hand and ducking under them, while remembering to do the steps and stand in the right place. But she'd soon got it right. Now, she felt proud to be stepping and turning with the French girls in a dance that made such pretty patterns.

The crowd applauded in delight, and Poppy could hear the clicking of hundreds of cameras. "I'm going to be in a lot of holiday photos!" she thought. Out of the corner of her eye she could see her family with Josette's mum and brother, all waving and smiling. And of course, Dad was filming everything.

The girls curtsied and left the centre of the square, applauded by the crowd. Relieved that she hadn't made a mistake, Poppy ran to stand with her family. Josette's mum kissed her on both cheeks. "Bravo!" she said. "Now, watch this!"

A group of men dressed in white, with red scarves, marched into the square. Some were teenage boys, some a little older. They danced in lines and circles, doing such fast, complicated steps that Poppy's eyes couldn't follow their feet. "Awesome!" she thought.

But she wasn't prepared for what happened next. The men began to kick their legs up almost as high as their heads. First one leg, then the other, all in a line, perfectly together. Poppy gasped, joining in with the loud applause. But her astonishment grew when two of the older men picked up the smallest of the teenage boys, who, lying as straight and stiff as a piece of wood, was twirled round

above the dancers' heads while the crowd
roared and stamped.

"Look at that!" exclaimed Tom, his eyes
almost popping out of his head.

Fabian laughed. "*Danse Basquaise* is good,
is it not?"

"It's amazing!" agreed Tom. He grinned at
Poppy and Josette. "And your flower dance
was brilliant too," he said.

Fabian told Josette what Tom had said.
To Poppy's surprise, Josette
kissed Tom, first on one
cheek, then the other.
Poppy thought she had
never seen her brother go so red,
or look so shy. Though she felt very proud of
him for being so nice to Josette, she couldn't
help laughing along with everyone else.

Josette said something to her mother, then she took Poppy's hand. "Sun-day," she said carefully.

Poppy nodded. "Yes, Sunday," she repeated.

"*Danse,*" said Josette, which was almost the same word as "dance".

"We dance on Sunday?" guessed Poppy.

"*Fleurs!*" said Josette, pointing to the paper garlands.

The word sounded like "flur". Poppy hesitated, not sure what Josette meant. "We dance with the flowers?" she suggested.

Josette pointed to Lucien, then to the other girls, then back to the garlands, and did a few little dance steps. "*La fête,*" she said. It sounded like "fette".

Poppy didn't understand, but Fabian

came to her rescue. "A fête is a festival,"
he explained. "Dancing, singing, eating,
drinking – for four days!"

"The festival is in Bayonne," added Mimi,
"a big town not far away. Lucien's dancers
will perform on the last day, Sunday. Will
you dance with them again, Poppy?"

"Can I?" Poppy asked her parents excitedly.

Dad looked at Mum, who nodded. "Well,"
he said to Poppy, "we'll be going to Bayonne
sometime on this holiday, so it might as well
be on Sunday."

"Yay!" exclaimed Poppy, slapping hands
with Tom.

"Yay!" repeated Josette, slapping hands with her brother, too.

Now it was Tom's turn to laugh. "We've taught Josette an English word," he said, "but it isn't even a proper word!"

Poppy grinned. "Everyone knows what it means, though," she replied. "It means 'I'm so happy' – and right now, I *am*!"

Festival Fireworks

Bayonne was a big town, with bridges over a river and a large square with a bandstand in the middle. All around the square hung red, black and green Basque flags, and little stalls sold hot food, pastries, sweets, drinks and Basque souvenirs.

"Look at all these people!" exclaimed Mum. "Hold my hand, Poppy, and Tom, stay with Dad. I've never seen such a crowd in my life!"

There was almost no space to walk between the men and women of all ages, teenagers, children and babies in pushchairs. And all of them, even the babies, were dressed in white trousers and white shirts, with red scarves around their middle.

Mimi had lots of these Basque costumes, which she had lent to Poppy's family. "You will be French for today!" she told them.

Tom didn't mind dressing up once he saw Fabian in the white costume. And when they got to Bayonne and he found he looked like everyone else, he was pleased. "This is so cool!" he said. "Can I go with Fabian and get a Coke?"

"Later," said Dad. "We've just got to get through this crowd, or the girls will be late for the dancing."

The display of Basque dancing was due to start at six o'clock. It had been a hot day, but now the sun was just beginning to sink behind the buildings, and soon dusk would fall upon the square. "In the night," said Fabian with a grin, "is very exciting!"

"What's going to happen?" asked Tom. "Fireworks?"

Fabian waggled his finger. "Surprise!" he teased.

Around the bandstand there was a space for dancing, with barriers for the crowd to stand behind.

When Poppy took her place for the garland dance she was astonished to see so many people, stretching around her in all directions, standing on balconies and leaning out of windows waving flags, and all dressed exactly the same. But when the dance started she forgot the audience, and concentrated on passing the garlands and doing her steps correctly. She didn't want to let Josette down on such an important occasion!

Lucien's high-kicking men caused an uproar so loud that Poppy had to cover her ears. She had never heard so many people shouting at once. "It's like a football match!" she said to Tom.

"Great, isn't it!" he replied, and roared with the others as the boy was spun round and round.

Other Basque dance groups performed next, sometimes with so many dancers they could hardly fit in the space. It looked spectacular, the women in their long skirts and lace caps, turning and stepping and jumping exactly in time with one another.

By the time the dance display was over, darkness had fallen and the lights in the square were on. But as Fabian had hinted, that was not the end of the celebrations. The Basque musicians left the bandstand, and their place was taken by men with guitars and trumpets. Another man sat down behind a large modern drum kit. The band adjusted amplifiers and microphones, and then the air was suddenly filled with a sound very familiar to Poppy's ears – Latin American dance music.

Couples crowded onto the dance floor, swinging and turning to the beat of the Latin music. No one could keep their feet still as the rhythm of the samba boomed all around them. "Come on, Josette!" cried Poppy. "I'll show you how!" And just like Josette had shown Poppy the garland dance, Poppy showed Josette the samba steps. The girls laughed as Josette stood on Poppy's toes a few times, but the French girl soon learnt what to do. People nearby started to copy them, and soon Poppy and Josette were samba-ing round the square, followed by a line of couples, both adults and children.

The band played a cha-cha-cha and a salsa, and Poppy showed Josette how to do those dances too. Like the samba, the salsa needed you to sway your hips, bounce on your feet and shake your shoulders. Josette looked almost like a real Latin American dancer, with her suntanned skin and her dark hair flipping as she salsa-ed.

The band began to play rock 'n' roll music. Lucien danced with Poppy's mum, and Josette's mum with Poppy's dad. Poppy and Josette stood at the side and watched them.

"They look good, don't they?" said Tom's voice behind Poppy.

As she turned
to answer him,
she found herself
showered with
hundreds of tiny pieces
of coloured paper. Some
of them even went in her
mouth. "Ugh!" she exclaimed. "Tom!
What are you *doing*?"

But then Fabian threw bits of paper all over
Josette. Poppy realized that all around them,
children were taking handfuls of
paper confetti,
just like you
throw at
weddings,
from bags
and scattering

68

them over other children – and sometimes
adults, too. The game was to throw your
bits of paper over someone before they did
it to you, and escape from them when they
chased you.

"*La bataille de confetti!*"
called Fabian. "Confetti
battle, yes?"

"Let the battle begin!"
said Tom, plunging
his hand into his
bag of confetti.

Josette ducked his throw, scooped up
some paper from a pile on
the ground and threw it over
him. Fabian hooted
with laughter
as Tom shook

confetti out of his hair, so Tom chucked his next handful over Fabian.

Rummaging in her pocket for coins, Josette led Poppy to one of the little wooden stalls beside the square. Poppy had thought they were selling sweets, but the bags on display turned out to be filled with confetti, in every colour Poppy could imagine. Josette bought two bags, gave one to Poppy and grinned mischievously.

"La bataille de confetti!" she said.

The confetti battle was mad, but such fun, that Poppy wished the bags of confetti would last for ever. Most of the confetti ended up on the ground, of course, so when the

children had no more money
they scooped up handfuls, or
even armfuls, and threw it over
each other. The confetti got
dirtier and dirtier, and so did
all the white trousers and
white tops.

"Goodness,
look at the state
of you!" said Mum. "We'll never get all that
confetti out of your hair!" She didn't sound
cross, though.

Poppy knew she must look very messy,
but she was having such
a great time, she didn't
care. "Can we come
again next year?"
she asked Mum.

Mum and Dad looked at each other. "That depends on Jill and Simon," said Dad. "We need them to run the hotel."

"And look after Lucky," added Mum.

Lucky was Poppy's puppy, who lived with Auntie Jill and Uncle Simon.

Suddenly, for the first time since they'd left England, Poppy missed Lucky's velvety coat and brown eyes, and his busy little tail. "I hope Lucky's all right!" she said.

"Of course he is," said Mum. She caught sight of something, and pointed. "What's *that*?" she asked.

The confetti battle was over, and people were watching while the final preparations for the fireworks were being made. Inside the barriers, where the dancing had been, two men were wheeling a very strange object into place. Poppy stared and stared.

The thing on wheels looked a bit like a narrow picnic table, but with pieces of wood nailed on to represent a neck, a horned head and a tail. All over it, attached by wires, were unlit fireworks. "Wow!" gasped Tom, who was just as amazed as Poppy. "It's a *bull*!"

"It's called the Toro de Fuego," said Mimi. "It's Spanish. It means 'bull of fire'. Just wait till they light it!"

There was an announcement, in which Poppy heard the words *"Toro de Fuego"*, and then the band began to play, the crowd began to cheer, and the fireworks on the bull were lit. One of the men ran round and round inside the barrier, pulling the fizzing, sparkling, exploding "bull of fire" after him on a string. The fireworks went off in all directions, skidding along the ground, soaring into the sky, whooshing and spinning around the bull's horns and tail. It was very spectacular, and a tiny bit scary too!

Then, just as the Toro de Fuego finished his parade and was wheeled off, the screeching sound of fireworks began, and the sky was filled with colour and light.

It was breathtaking. More and more fireworks were lit, making deafening bangs and lighting up the faces of the spectators. It was the best firework display Poppy had ever seen, even better than the one in Brighton every year on the fifth of November.

Tom must have been thinking the same thing. "Brighton's going to be a bit dull after all this, isn't it?" he said as the crowd applauded an especially loud rocket.

Poppy knew what he meant, though she thought she'd be just as happy at home. "I like it here," she told her brother, "but I'm *so* looking forward to telling Zack and Mia all about it, and playing with Lucky, and going to Miss Johnson's classes again."

Tom smiled. "You and your dancing," he said. He brushed some confetti out of Poppy's hair. "You look a sight, you know."

"So do you," said Poppy, looking at the dirt smeared on Tom's face and the dust on his white clothes. But although he was dirty, Poppy thought she had never seen him look so happy.

When the firework display was over they went to a pavement café for drinks. Poppy had never been outdoors so late at night

before! She heard the people around her chattering in French, and the last strains of music from the square. She smelled coffee and cigarette smoke, and the sweet smell of the drinks in little glasses that people had with their coffee. A machine like a vacuum cleaner on wheels had begun to clear up the confetti from the square. The men were dismantling the scaffolding that had held the fireworks, and the drummer was packing up his drum kit.

Today had been very special.

"Josette," said Poppy, and Josette turned to her with a "yes?" expression. Her hair was also covered with confetti, and a piece was still stuck on her cheek. Poppy wanted to tell her that this was all thanks to her and the garland dance, but she didn't know how.

All she could remember was the word for "thank you".

"*Merci*," she said shyly.

Josette was pleased to hear Poppy speaking French. "*Ah, merci!*" she cried, and gave Poppy a kiss on her cheek. Poppy liked the way French people were always kissing each other. She was so glad that Josette was her friend!

She leaned across the table to Fabian. "What's the word for friend?" she asked.

"*Amie*," he said.

"*A-mee*," said Poppy, copying how he said it.

"Very good," he said.

Poppy leaned back to Josette. "Amie," she said, pointing to herself, then to Josette.

"*Amie!*" squealed Josette in delight.

Poppy was sure that even after the holiday was over, and everyone was getting on with their usual lives, Josette would never forget how she and Poppy had done Latin American dancing in the square. And even if she never came back to the Basque area of France again, Poppy would always remember the Toro de Fuego, the fireworks, the red, white and black costumes – and especially her friend, Josette.

Natasha May loves dance of all kinds. When she was a little girl she dreamed of being a dancer, but also wanted to be a writer. "So writing about dancing is the best job in the world," she says. "And my daughter, who is a dancer, keeps me on my toes about the world of dance."

Shelagh McNicholas loves to draw people spinning around and dancing. Her passion began when her daughter, Molly, started baby ballet classes, "and as she perfected her dancing skills we would practise the jive, samba and quickstep all around the house!"